PUFFIN BOOKS

Santa's Diary

It was a cold frosty Christmas Eve last year, and I went outside hoping to see the pole star in the night sky. As I looked up I saw a comet streaking right across the sky.

It was a very unusual comet. It looked as if it were chasing after (or was being pulled along by) a team of flying reindeer!

Then suddenly there was a thump at my feet, a Ho Ho Ho in the sky and in the blink of an eyelid the comet had disappeared. I looked down, and there on the ground was a diary. It seemed to have fallen out of the sky. It could only belong to one person . . . Santa!

Had Santa dropped it by mistake, or had he wanted you all to read it? This is something we'll never know, but as Santa loves sharing all his toys with girls and boys, I'm sure he would not mind one little bit if you all read his diary. After all, when you discover just how hard he works, you'll be amazed – I was!

And so here it is for the first time ever, for everyone to read and enjoy . . . the one and only Santa's Diary.

Shoo Rayner

D0522864

Also by Shoo Rayner
The Christmas Stocking Joke Book

Santa's Diary

Shoo Rayner

PUFFIN BOOKS

PUFFIN BOOKS

Published by the Penguin Group
27 Wrights Lane, London W8 5TZ, England
Viking Penguin Inc., 40 West 23rd Street, New York, New York 10010, USA
Penguin Books Australia Ltd, Ringwood, Victoria, Australia
Penguin Books Canada Ltd, 2801 John Street, Markham, Ontario, Canada L3R 1B4
Penguin Books (NZ) Ltd, 182–190 Wairau Road, Auckland 10, New Zealand

Penguin Books Ltd, Registered Offices: Harmondsworth, Middlesex, England

First published 1990
1 3 5 7 9 10 8 6 4 2

Copyright © Shoo Rayner, 1990
All rights reserved

The moral right of the author has been asserted

Printed by Clays Ltd, St Ives plc
Filmset in Palatino 12 on $13\frac{1}{2}$

For
Santa
from
an admirer!

Year Planner

JANUARY_____ 9th Holiday — back 31st
Bliss! Sonshine! Can't wait!

FEBRUARY_____ 14th Valentine's Day —
(don't forget!) 29th remember
it's a leap Year!

MARCH_____ 1st Back to work.
27th The Big Decision

APRIL_____ 17th off to TOY FAIR —
19th to Norway 29th Return —
Put Reindeer out to pasture.

MAY_____ Office re-organisation.

JUNE_____ 5th to Australia —
9th to North America — 12th Home.
18th MY BIRTHDAY !!!

JULY _Interviews for the Santa University start. Begin lectures._

AUGUST _Expect first present lists_
8th _Grand opening of the NEW SYSTEM_

SEPTEMBER 3rd _Sleigh in for Service_
10th _Graduation Day —_
21st _Mrs C's Birthday_

OCTOBER _1st Reindeer round up —_
— Training Sessions —
12th _Choose α and β teams —_

NOVEMBER _1st Wedding Anniversary._
9th _Start World Tour opening department stores._ 30th _Home_

DECEMBER 24th _BIG DELIVERY!!_
25th _Christmas Day._
31st _NEW YEAR'S EVE_

7

Personal Details

Name   *S. Claus*

Address   *Icicles*
            The Tundra
            Iceboro
            North Pole

Zip/Postcode *NP 1*   Telephone No. *Tundra 1*

Occupation   *Benefactor*

Marital status *Married*   Blood Group *DD+ neg*

Next of Kin *Mrs Sandy Claus*
            (address as above)

Sleigh No. *0179 /321/B/0002*

Bank   *Northminster International*

Suit Size   *42*

Lawyers   *Oldham & Grabbitt*

Elf Service *MU2 /UB/3197/D*

Season Ticket No. *NBT/2716/B/ off peak.*

If found please publish!

Useful Addresses

Name **Merryweather**
the OFFICE
North Pole   Telephone   Tundra 2

Name **Kurt Antlerson (Vet)**
St Rudolph's Veterinary Hospital
North Pole   Telephone   Tundra 5

Name **While-u-wait sleigh Repairs,** (Rod Axelson)
Toboggan Row.
North Pole   Telephone   Tundra 3.

Name **Pola Pizza (home delivery)**
Pepperoni Ave.
North Pole   Telephone   Tundra 17

Name **Dr Say R. Pleece. MD.**
Centre for Coughs & sneezes.
North Pole   Telephone   Tundra 13

Name **Bobby Bristlethwaite**
Beard Barber. High st.
North pole   Telephone   Tundra 7

January

1 January

I was just folding up my red suit today (which Mrs Claus says is too damp and should be aired first, before it's put away!), when a parcel fell out of the pocket and on to the floor. And this is what was inside. A diary!

Now, I last wore my suit on Christmas Eve, so that's when I must have put it in my pocket. Christmas Eve is really quite busy for me and, what with all those drinks and cookies that people leave out for me, I can quite forget which continent I'm in!

But now I do remember! Yes, that lovely wrapping paper must have been drawn by hand. All those lovely reindeer on it.

Yummy ORANGE JUICE!

Yummy COOKIES!

for Santa from an admirer.!

I wonder who this secret admirer is ....?

Anyway, now I've started writing in it I'd better carry on. I know . . . I can take it with me on holiday. Just think of it . . . three weeks of sun, sea and sand – that's my idea of bliss!!!

What to take on holiday

Mrs Claus! √
5 T-shirts √
2 Bermuda shorts √
5 underpants √
Camera √
Film √
Jacket √
Guidebook/map √
Phrasebook √
Sneakers √
Beach shoes √
Beach towels √
Suntan lotion √
Sunglasses √
DIARY!! √
Pens & pencils √
AIRPLANETICKETS!! √
PASSPORTS!! √
Money √
Teabags √
Sunhat √
Toothbrush, toothpaste, hairbrush, beardbrush, shampoo and protein cream rinse √
Shirt & tie (in case there's somewhere smart to go!) √
That red thing with the blue whatsit in the bottom drawer of the bureau √

Things to do

*Put reindeer out

*Check that there's enough cat food in the freezer

*Stop Newspaper deliveries

*Stop Milk delivery

Books to read

The Electronic Revolution by Mike Roe √

The Truth about Santa! by Liza Lott √

9 January

6 p.m. Very bored. Mrs Claus and I have been at the airport now for six hours. Iceberg 'There's more to us than meets the eye' Airways had us checking in at midday, only to tell us that they can't find the plane! I'll say there's more to them than meets the eye! How can anyone be so useless that they can lose an aeroplane? I ask you.

8 p.m. Still no sign of the plane. Have finished reading *The Truth about Santa!* I have never read so much rubbish in all my life. How people are allowed to make up stories about me I just don't know! And why do people refuse to believe that I exist? It makes life so difficult for me.

9 p.m. *Still* no sign of the plane! Have been reading *The Electronic Revolution* by Mike Roe. Merryweather, my personal assistant, gave it to me. I don't understand a word of it. If it hadn't been a present I would have torn it up into a thousand tiny bits (or are they bites?)

10 p.m. They've found the plane under a snowdrift! How can anyone lose a jumbo jet under a snowdrift? Beats me!

1 a.m. Very, *very* tired. However, we are now in our seats. Tomorrow we'll be in the sunshine. Hooray! Sleep now.

← what a load of rubbish.'

13

10 January

7 a.m. Woke up still on aeroplane. Looked outside window. Snow everywhere! Big friendly lights spell out the message:

ICEBERG AIRWAYS WELCOME YOU
TO NORTH POLE INTERNATIONAL

and then in small print all the guff about 'there's more to us than meets the eye'! They'll be black eyes if they don't watch out!!! It turns out that we haven't taken off yet!!

8 a.m. Well, the thing was that since they couldn't find the plane last night, they gave us the food trays that we would have eaten on the plane. Once we got on the plane they couldn't take off because there wasn't any breakfast on board. Meanwhile the chef had disappeared and has only just been located!

BREAKFAST!!!!

BAKED ALASKA!

SALT

PEPPER POT (full of salt!)

NASTY, WET, SMELLY FINGER WIPE!

FRIGO SMELL

POLA COLA

SMELLY OLD REINDEER CHEESE

ICE CREAM

ICE BURGER

FRENCH FRIES

"E-ZEE" BREAK KNIFE & FORK.

9 a.m. Breakfast is on board and we are taxiing down the runway. My tummy feels funny. Either I am very hungry or these seatbelts aren't big enough!

31 January

Iceberg Tours will be hearing from my lawyers!
We are back home at last, no thanks to Iceberg Airways.
I was waiting for them to try and tell us they couldn't
find the plane because it had melted in the sun!!!

Sun!! Hah! That's another thing. It's rained solidly for
three weeks! They call it the sunshine coast and what
does it do for three weeks? It rains.

That's only part of it though. I work jolly hard
throughout the year, and I look forward to my holiday,
and so does Mrs Claus. We booked a nice big apartment
with a sea view, and what do we get? A tiny little room
at the back with a view of the oil refinery.

Did I say oil refinery? Look at these two photographs.

Picture A is the one they use in the travel brochure and on the postcards. Doesn't it look lovely? Just the place for a holiday? Well, picture B is the other half of the picture that they don't put on the postcards. Thanks to the oil refinery, and the drilling rigs in the bay, the beach is covered in oil! So . . . No sunbathing . . . No swimming!

What about the hotel swimming pool? 'Very sorry, sir, it's out of season. Pool closed for maintenance.' Everything was out of season!! The weather, the shops, the cinema, the disco. Of course I couldn't go sailboarding because of the oil in the sea and when I wanted to go hang-gliding instead they tried to tell me I was too old . . . Ha!

I told them: 'Do you know who I am? I'm Santa Claus and I've spent more time flying around than you've done breathing!'

You can't win. People either don't believe in you, in which case they just laugh when you tell them who you are. Or, if they do believe in you, they don't believe that Santa would be hang-gliding, in which case they think you're crazy, in which case they call the police, which is how I spent three days of my holiday in prison, because they didn't believe I was who I said I was. They thought my passport was forged!! They let me go in the end, only because Mrs Claus told them I was soft in the head!!!

February

1 February

Well! Not such a bad picture of Mrs Claus's sun-hat with palm tree in background. I have been known to take worse pictures! As for the rest of the holiday snaps, well . . .

The man at Polarkwik ('We make memories for you!') says that I have got oil and sand in my camera and that after I took the above photo the whole works jammed up. So all the pictures I took on holiday are on the same piece of film, which just comes out white when printed!

I wouldn't mind, but there was documentary evidence on that film of all the disasters that happened on holiday.

2 February
Went to see Oldham & Grabbitt, the old firm of family
lawyers (Motto: We never give up).

They say that Iceberg Airways and Iceberg Tours have
treated us terribly. Not to worry about the photographs —
they would have been very useful, but they will start
proceedings to sue Iceberg for giving me and Mrs Claus
such a terrible holiday.

3 February
I hate February. It's just cold and wet and grey and
boring. February! Oh my goodness! I mustn't forget that
it's St Valentine's Day on the 14th. Mrs Claus will be so
upset if I forget.

6 February
Did large pussy-cat jigsaw. Don't forget St Valentine's
Day!!!

9 February
Received letter from lawyers. They have sent a strongly
worded letter to both Iceberg Airways and Iceberg Tours.
I should think so too! Mustn't forget the 14th!

11 February
Lawyers heard from Iceberg Tours. They deny everything!
HAH! Don't forget Valentine's Day!

12 February
Lawyers heard from Iceberg Airways. They deny
everything! HAH! How can they deny losing a jumbo jet
for a few hours? Lawyers writing stronger letter.
(Remember 14th!)

13 February

It would be Friday the thirteenth, wouldn't it? Merryweather, my dear and trusted secretary and Elf Friday, phones up and says there's a panic in the office and would I come over immediately?

He knows that I'm not due back at the office until next month so I assume it must be serious to call me out.

This is a Wijit. Actually, it is two halves of a Wijit.

And what is a Wijit? I hear you say.

Well, a Wijit is the left-handed part of the thing that holds together most of the toys that are made up here in the North Pole.

We order and use millions of them every year. We've always had them from the Norwegian trolls and dwarves before. Last year I gave half the order to a new firm of pixies who said they could make Wijits for half the price.

Of course Merryweather advised me against using the pixies. He said they couldn't produce the quality. He was right!

Pixie Products Inc.

14 February

What a complete mess! The thing that hurts is that it's all my own fault. I was on the telephone half the night trying to find a pixie to take responsibility for the poor quality of their workmanship.

Eventually this pixie called Catskill came on the line. He tried to tell me that the Wijits that they had delivered were acceptable within the tolerances set on the order form. TOLERANCES! I can tell you I lost my tolerance. I started shouting down the phone, telling this aforementioned Catskill that if I ever got hold of him I'd . . .

Luckily, Merryweather grabbed the phone at that moment, so I never got to tell him exactly what I would have done with him had I caught him. Merryweather was none too pleased with me for losing my temper. 'Just think how this would ruin the public's image of you, if it were to get out.' I have to agree, if those pixies really wanted to make mischief they could sell the story to the newspapers. I can just see the headlines now . . . SANTA LOSES RAG . . . SANTA IN PIXIE PICKLE . . . SANTA IN FIDGET OVER PIXIE WIJIT . . . And so on!

Anyway, this morning I had to go back into the office bright and early. The reason being that the Norwegian trolls and dwarves start work early and are generally in a good mood first thing in the morning. The favour I was going to ask of them would need them to be in a good mood too!

AAAAAARRRRGH! It has just dawned on me. Today was Valentine's Day! Well, it was yesterday really, since I've only just got back home from the office and it's the early hours of tomorrow already while I'm writing up what happened yesterday! Mrs Claus has gone to bed. No doubt she is in a bad mood with me too.

Anyway, where was I? Oh yes, as you can imagine the trolls and dwarves were not very pleased with me coming back and asking them to double the production of Wijits. Well, after I halved their order from last year I'm not surprised. I had to send a grovelling apology to them and a glowing testimonial in praise of their 'legendary workmanship'.

What that means is that next year they will be too busy to work for me or they will have doubled their prices.

I can just see the adverts:

N.T.&D. Engineers
—Trondheim·on·sea—

Unsolicited Testimonials:
"legendary Workmanship"
(Santa)
"Such quality"
(Santa)

WIJITS OUR SPECIALITY!

purveyors of Wijits to Santa Claus. "No one else can match them..."

16 February

Well! I just don't know. By the time I realized I had forgotten Valentine's Day it was Sunday and too late to get a card. So I drew one like this.

Oh my darling little Sandy

I hope you don't get too irate

Sweetness you're my sugar candy

Hope you don't mind if the card's a bit late!

I know I'm not very good at poetry, never have been, but I don't know why she's not talking to me. She'll drive me potty with all this silence. Can't wait for the end of the month so that I can go back to work full time!

29 February

She would pick a leap year to go silent on me, wouldn't she? I can't wait for February to be over!

March

1 March
Golly, it's nice to be back at the office! Mrs Claus is still not talking to me so it's great to be back in the driving seat, finger on the pulse, taking command ready to start another year's countdown to Christmas.

Of course, since Merryweather's been here it's been a bit easier. He keeps the office open for the first two quiet months of the year. He's so willing, but I know he's really rather glad to have me back in the office, to take control of the everyday running of things.

He keeps hovering around me trying to say something. He's obviously too emotional just to simply say 'welcome back'!

It's funny though – he asked me if Mrs Claus has spoken to me yet. How does he know that she's not talking to me?

I've had enough of all this nonsense. I'll call Mrs Claus right now . . .

. . . Well, she talked to me! And she agreed to come out with me tonight for a romantic evening at Polapizza. Oh, I know how to please her. She turns to jelly just at the thought of all that exotic pepperoni, olives and gooey mozzarella cheese! It reminds her of one of our better holidays!

2 March
Speechless!

3 March
Still speechless!!!

4 March
All right . . . this is what happened. I picked up Mrs Claus and we went off to Polapizza, where I'd reserved a quiet little corner table for two. Mrs Claus seemed to have buried the hatchet. We laughed and joked and enjoyed our pizzas until I thought that, at last, everything was back to normal again . . . that's when she told me that I ought to retire! Me! HAH! Anyone would think I was getting too old for the job! Hah!

To cap it all she says that Merryweather could quite easily take over now. He might have to wear a couple of pillows under the red suit, but she thinks he's very capable.

Very capable indeed! Do you know what Merryweather looks like?

This is a recent photo of him. Now really, does he look full of Ho Ho Ho?

Of course not. Why, he hasn't even got a beard!

5 March

Well, I decided to visit the office today. There was Merryweather, hovering around trying to say something. 'WELL?' I said in my loudest, gruffest voice. 'What is it?'

Merryweather asked me if I'd read *The Electronic Revolution*, that he gave me to read on holiday. I told him that it was all gobbledygook! Then, with a pained expression on his face, he began to tell me how we need to get computerized!

'I suppose you agree with Mrs Claus, that I should retire and you take over?' I said. But surprisingly enough he seemed quite shocked at the idea. He said that he had explained to Mrs Claus that the work-load was getting impossible to handle and would she have a word with me about getting in some help. He'd never thought that she'd ask me to retire!

7 March

I have asked Merryweather to prepare a report on the state of the business. He is beavering away, working out his figures on one of those useless wristwatch calculators we had left over last year. No wonder he wears glasses . . . he has to tap the numbers in with a matchstick!

10 March

Merryweather is still hard at work. Goodness knows what he's up to! Meanwhile, this year's toy catalogues are starting to arrive. Great fun looking at them!

18 March
This is it. Merryweather's Report!

TOWARDS A NEW CENTURY
A report into the efficiency
of Santa Industries Inc.
by Hubert Merryweather

The efficiency of Christmas Eve deliveries has seriously deteriorated over the past few decades for various reasons.

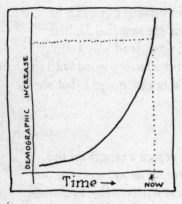

The demographic time shift
Since Christmas Eve deliveries started, the number of deliveries has been in direct proportion to the number of believers.

Now the number of believers are not only more widely spread but there are just more people in the world!

The production problem
With so many deliveries to make there follows a production problem. Do we spread the same amount further (i.e. decrease the present-to-stocking ratio) or do we increase production?

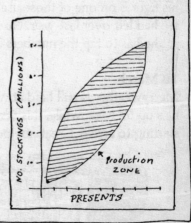

26

Unless the PSR (present-to-stocking ratio) is to start falling (I might remind you of paragraph 86 clause b of our charter which says that no child should be disappointed without very good reason), drastic action needs to be taken.

1. All records should be computerized immediately.
2. New warehouses with in-plant paper recycling and automatic present-wrapping machines should be built immediately in strategic worldwide sites.
3. A new Santa University should be started to train Santa's helpers properly. In this day and age Santa cannot reasonably be expected to be everywhere at the same time.
4. Personal appearances: Santa will have to delegate some responsibility to 'doubles' if he is to keep his strength up for the ever-increasing burden of Christmas Eve deliveries.
5. The office should make use of all the modern innovations in technology. Fax machines would be very useful. (The post here is somewhat erratic!)

All this will help take the weight of worry off Santa's shoulders. (However broad they are, there are limits.) This will mean that Santa can be his usual, happy, Ho Ho Ho self, in the knowledge that everything is running sweetly and smoothly back at head office!

Hubert Merryweather.

19 March
Well, I've read it all and a lot of it makes sense. There's more to Merryweather than I thought.

27 March

We've talked it all through and Merryweather is absolutely right. I didn't know that he was doing so much work. Come to that, I didn't know that *I* was doing so much work.

I'm going to carry on with Christmas as we know it, while Merryweather puts all the new plans into operation. We have ordered three new waste paper recycling plants with The Christmas Gift Wrap Printer Option, to be delivered by the end of August in our new international depots in Europe, America and Australia. This is how it works:

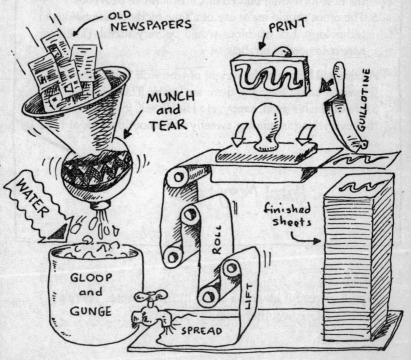

SCHEMATIC DIAGRAM OF RECYCLED PAPER PLANT

April

3 April

Merryweather continues to organize everything. He says it would be better if I were to get out and about for most of the month.

It would be a good idea to go and visit the Norwegian dwarves and trolls. After all that Wijit business it would show willing if I were to go and tell them how much they are appreciated. Now I come to think of it, the International Toy Fair starts at the end of next week. Judging by the catalogues I've received, there are a few interesting things to see this year. Maybe I should take Mrs Claus with me. After the long, dark, cold winter (and the Valentine's Day disaster!), I think maybe she would appreciate a proper holiday.

5 April

Well, as you can imagine, after the last holiday, I am not very pleased with Iceberg Tours. So I went down to Aurora 'The sky's the limit' Tours this morning to fix up the travel schedule.

Life would be so much easier if I could just hitch up the reindeer to the sleigh and fly off on my own, but the poor dears do need their rest. Besides which, it would never do to be seen flying around in the middle of April! So it's plain Mr Claus going to the Toy Fair again. No one would believe me if I told them who I really was, and if they did believe me they would double the price of everything!

17 April

Golly! I always forget just how much fun the Toy Fair is! I'm not sure what Mrs Claus is up to, but I've been having a rare old time.

Every famous toy maker in the world and, or so it seems, every crackpot inventor in the world is here too! These are some of the weird things that I saw.

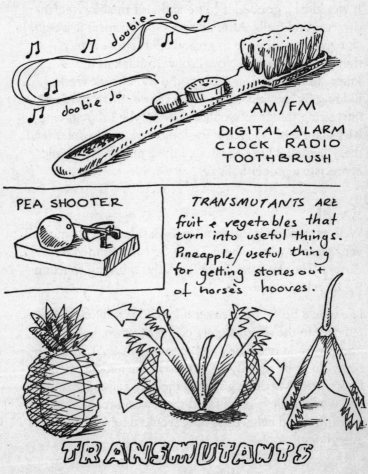

doobie-do
doobie do

AM/FM
DIGITAL ALARM
CLOCK RADIO
TOOTHBRUSH

PEA SHOOTER

TRANSMUTANTS ARE fruit & vegetables that turn into useful things. Pineapple / useful thing for getting stones out of horse's hooves.

TRANSMUTANTS

PEDAL POLICE CAR

WITH MOTORWAY INCIDENT OPTIONS.

THE ACME HELPING HAND (GETS straight to the point)

THE ACME CUDDLY BRICK

WAAAAAH!

CRY BABY!

- It feels real.
- It wets itself.
- It soils its nappies.
- It cries all night!

(batteries not included)

31

18 April

Now I know what Mrs Claus has been up to. She seems to have bought half the town!

You can't 'do' the Toy Fair in a day, so Mrs Claus has made the most of it. I got back to the hotel this evening, and I could hardly get in the room for shopping bags and parcels. In the middle of the room, rustling away under a pile of tissue paper was Mrs Claus, who, it seemed, was determined to try on everything she had bought!

She'd bought me a present though. Said it was a bargain, what with it being so out of season. A lovely set of Christmas patterned thermal underwear. They're very warm and with all those Christmas trees all over them they should keep me warm on Christmas Eve!

As for everything else, I'm sure that we'll be over our luggage weight allowance at the airport. That is if we can get all this packed by tomorrow! We've got to catch that flight to Norway. Can't go and let the dwarves and trolls down again. We'd never get them to say hello let alone make Wijits!

19 April

We needed two taxis to get us to the airport. Apart from the obvious things like clothes, we have got, hidden at the bottom of our suitcases, a Wok, at least three knitted ballerinas that fit over toilet rolls, several Filofaxes and all the bits to go inside (which Merryweather asked for specially). Since Merryweather convinced Mrs C. that I was going into semi-retirement there is nothing she won't do for him!

We've got books, cake tins, food processors and an awful lot of stuff that says either 'designer' or 'lifestyle' on the label. It all looks like a load of rubbish to me but who cares? We are on holiday, aren't we?

20 April

Have I been asleep for the last ten years or what? The trolls and dwarves tell me it's been that long since I visited last. I don't believe it. Everything is passing me by. These guys could make a year's supply of Wijits in a couple of weeks. No more of that hammer and anvil stuff. They've got fully automated, computer-controlled Wijit-making machines!

And that's not all. Now that they've got their production speeded up, they've had time to invent new things, like their remarkable instant mug-making machine. Put a photo in the machine and it prints it on to the mug like so:

Unfortunately we didn't know that a photo was being taken at the time so the mug didn't come out too well. Quite a good shot of Mrs C.'s new hat!

27 April
It really is quite remarkable what these chaps have done since I was last here. Those old, dark, dank fiordside caves have been transformed into bright, airy, hitec, light industrial premises.

It makes me realize that Merryweather has his finger on the pulse. I can hardly wait to get home to see what changes he's made to the office.

28 April
On our way home. I'm so glad we didn't go with Iceberg Tours. Must see how the lawyers are doing.

30 April
Put reindeer out to pasture.

May

1 May

Popped into Oldham & Grabbitt. They'd heard from
Iceberg Airways, who admitted that they were in the
wrong to lose their Jumbo in a snow-drift and would I
accept a discount voucher for the next time I fly Iceberg
Airways?

Well, I'm not proud! That suits me just fine. As for Iceberg
Tours, they have offered Mrs Claus and myself another
holiday next January where there aren't oil rigs and where
the sun really shines. They were also very sorry that my
camera had clogged up on the beach and would I accept
the instant Polaroid camera enclosed in lieu?

I'll say I would! There's nothing quite like a good lawyer
when you need one.

Gave Merryweather a call. He says that everything will
be ready for me to come into the office on the 4th.

4 May

Well, I really can't believe it! Merryweather has
transformed the place. The old office with its bulging
filing cabinets and stacks of paper, not to mention the
peeling wallpaper, has been turned into a gleaming,
humming, technological hive of industry! It has been
redecorated and filled up with new staff. Elves and fairies
everywhere. Merryweather has shown me how to use my
new camera . . .

LARRY, ON RECEPTION →

← THE COMPUTER

MY 'STAFF'!!

← MERRYWEATHER PLACING AN ORDER!

10 May

It really is quite extraordinary what Merryweather has done in the office. All that technology is quite incredible. Our suppliers can send us pictures of what they are making for us over the telephone by using something called a Fax machine.

We can write out our orders and send them to our suppliers on the Fax too. They get our orders in seconds now, whereas, even using express mail, you could never be sure when a letter would arrive. Well, you just can't trust the mail any more, can you?

All those filing cabinets have gone as well. It's all on disc now. Quite how they do it I just don't know, but all our records for the last two hundred years are now on ten small pieces of plastic! Merryweather showed me what you can do with them.

By fiddling around with something he calls a mouse, he can work out deliveries three years ahead, all based on the 'Plotting of Demographic Data'. Where did he learn all this stuff from? It certainly wasn't at Pole Street Elven Infants School!

21 May

Here is a photo of the new Santa University after I'd laid the foundation stone.

oops! finger over lens!

I know it doesn't look much but it makes me feel so proud to see it taking shape. You cannot imagine how difficult personal appearances have got recently.

In the old days I only had to pose occasionally for artists who were designing Christmas cards, and then do the big delivery on Christmas Eve. In those days, when children wanted to ask me for something, they would write me a letter and send it up the chimney. Of course they don't make chimneys like they used to, so I have to nip round the department stores to meet my public. As you can imagine, this is very tiring so I'm going to get some help at last.

29 May

Merryweather says that we can start advertising for Santas! The University building is coming along so well that we can think about getting our first crop of students in this summer.

People expect to see me at department stores, and why not? But a little knowledge of arithmetic would make them wonder how on earth I manage to be in all of them at the same time! Well, I do have some tricks I can play with the space-time continuum, but asking me to be in *every* store puts a bit of a strain on me. Asking me to be in every store *and* be jolly and Ho ho hoey at the same time, is pushing back the very limits of physical possibility!

So we are advertising for kindly old people to be Santa's helpers who will pretend to be me. That's what we need the University for. My helpers will be so well trained, no one will ever know that they aren't me! So after I come riding into town to open the grotto, one of my helpers can take over while I go off to open up somewhere else.

This may seem like a bit of a cheat but the point is that we need to know what is required in each stocking. To do that we need to get out and about and ask those who are going to get stockings what they would like in them! Otherwise we are in such a rush that we just have to put what we think is wanted into stockings. Sometimes we get it very wrong too!

June

2 June

Here is the advertisement. The art department have been working on it for a few days. (Did I mention that we've got our own art department now? That's progress for you.)

I know it doesn't look that brilliant but apparently it is designed to appeal to the kind of person we are looking for.

What will you do this Christmas when your garden is put to bed?

Come and do a useful and satisfying job with us.
(FULL TRAINING)

P.O. Box 1

It will appear in small local newspapers close to articles on gardening. This is because the kind of person we are looking for is the kind of person who is interested in gardening.

Why not have great big flashy advertisements? Well, you may ask . . . the thing is that we don't want to give the whole game away.

By putting the advertisement next to the gardening we will screen out the people that we don't want to apply for the job. Since, on the whole, children are not very interested in gardening they won't see the ad and wonder about it either.

5 June

Well, I've cashed in my Iceberg Airways discount voucher and I'm flying off on a quick round-the-world tour of our new international depots, Australia first.

6 June

Arrived safe and sound but it was a long journey. I'd still rather go by reindeer! Anyway, things are moving on apace here. The warehouses are going up in the middle of the desert, which makes it quite difficult to keep them a secret. We have set up a false company called 'KANGACAC'. This, we tell everyone, is a company that grows cactuses. It's so stupid, most people believe us! Anyone wanting a job here or more information is told that we will be growing cactuses here, in the sheds, and that since they are very slow-growing cactuses it will be at least fifty years until we harvest any. They think we're totally mad but that doesn't bother us!

Merryweather will come out soon to recruit local elves and fairies to help with the big wrap. The foundations, on which will stand the paper recycling plant (with gift wrap option), have been poured and are setting. It's all very exciting.

The recycled paper people are sworn to secrecy about the whole project. They will deliver machines to the three depots and get them running for us. After that we will run them but they will be in charge of gathering up waste paper for us, and will keep us supplied with ink for the printer.

9 June

On the American continent. This is such a secret location that I daren't even tell my own diary where I am! Suffice to say that it is not in the United States. The site for this depot is incredible. It is right inside a mountain. In the bad old days when everyone was trying to blow each other to bits with atom bombs and suchlike, the U.S. Army dug the inside of this mountain out so as to hide their early-warning radar systems. Well, they don't seem to need them as much as they did, so we have leased the mountain off the U.S. Government on very good terms. Well, what on earth are they going to do with a hollow mountain nowadays?

The other thing is that no one lives within a hundred miles of here, except for elves and fairies, but no one ever sees them. Anyway, they are going to come and work for us, so that works out just dandy.

12 June

Back home again. Iceberg Airways did their stuff and treated me like a VIP. Well, I should think so too. I *am* a VIP! Anyway, they didn't lose the plane this trip! Ha Ha!!

Ah! I don't think I mentioned that after due consideration, we decided to keep the European depot up here at the North Pole.

There seems to be nowhere left in Europe that we could build a giant warehouse without everybody knowing about it. So we are expanding the old Ice House up here.

18 June

WELL . . .! I was all set to go and visit the Ice House today, not really thinking about much, just going along to see how preparations were going. Merryweather had told me that the first parts of the paper plant were being assembled and would I like to watch.

Mrs Claus was in a fearful bustle and said that she had to get down to the shops early. She was acting very suspiciously if you ask me, and I was right.

I arrived at the Ice House to find that I couldn't get in! When I rang the bell Merryweather came out and gave me a credit card. I have to put this card into a slot that reads the card to check who I am. I then have to press in a number, which I have to keep secret, before the door opens automatically. It's all to provide increased security, says Merryweather. I don't know who we are keeping secure from, hidden away up here as we are!

Anyway, Merryweather showed me round the new front offices with the computer terminals connected to head office and all the department store grottos. He explained everything in the finest detail. How the warehousing was all based on a barcode system, which tells the computer exactly how much wrapping paper is required and so on and so on. He made me quite dizzy . . . which is why it was such a shock when the lights came on in the central packing hall . . .

I'd quite forgotten . . . It's My Birthday!!!
No one else had, it seems. The central packing hall is
where we've done our packing as long as I can remember.
Merryweather has had it dug out even more. It used to
be the most enormous room, carved out of the ice, and now
it's even bigger! And it was filled with elves and fairies
and a few visiting trolls and dwarves and the people who
are putting in the paper plant and Mrs Claus, of course,
all shouting . . . SURPRISE!! . . . HAPPY BIRTHDAY!!!!

Merryweather said that they were going to install new
barcoded shelving units tomorrow, so this was the last
time we could use the whole of the central packing hall.
Y'know, I'm beginning to wonder if all this
computerization is going to his head!

They had lots of presents for me: thick woolly socks, red
spotted handkerchiefs, smelly things for the bath and lots
of nice chocolatey things to eat. Mrs Claus gave me
'something for the man who has everything' – an in-sleigh
CD player and radio telephone. She's getting keen on
electronics too! And Merryweather, bless him, had knitted
me a new red hat and scarf to keep me warm this
Christmas. Wonders will never cease. He must have got a
'How to Knit' computer program!

July

3 July
Iceberg Tours have sent me a copy of their winter sun
holiday brochure. It's full of lovely photographs of sunny
places around the world. The only problem is making
sure that they are still sunny in January.

I showed it to Merryweather and he said he'd get the
research department on to it. (Research department? Since
when did we have a research department?) Anyway,
they're going to check out the average rainfall and hours
of sun that the best looking resorts can expect in January.

5 July
Got all the holiday details. The research department has
given me the list of resorts in descending order of
suitability. The art department had a bit of fun. They
took one of the photos from the brochure and added on
what they thought might have been missed in the picture!

7 July

Started to receive replies to the advertisement for stand-in Santas. Obviously the ad didn't give too much away about the job, but the first few inquiries are really quite encouraging.

They don't know what kind of job they are applying for so we send them a questionnaire to fill in, which will tell us all about them. We also tell them that we would like to train the right people to do a 'Valuable job during the Christmas period which will involve meeting and dealing with the public. No previous experience necessary. Would really suit retired Gentleman.'

Merryweather and I have had a long conversation about women Santas. In theory we should be an equal opportunity employer. That means that we should have Santaesses in the department store grottos but in the end we decided that we would stick with tradition. After all, they are supposed to be *my* doubles!

We've had some strange letters in so far, from all over the world. Well, wherever we placed the advertisement. I'm sure that some of the writers are quite unsuitable for the job. Merryweather says it's no problem. The questions on the application form are designed to be read by computer. This will give us a complete 'personality profile' of each applicant. (I think he's turning into a computer!!)

APPLICATION FOR CHRISTMAS PERIOD EMPLOYMENT AND TRAINING WITH NORTH POLE ENTERPRISE CO. INC.

Name .....Burt Bungle.... Age ..72.... M/~~F~~ ✓

Address ......28 LONESOME RIDGE,....
.................ALBERQUIRKY,
.CRIMBLE ISLES... Zip/Postcode CH12BB

Please read questions 1 to 7 and circle your answer
A, B or C

1 Would you rather be A. The Pope (B). The Queen of
England or C. The President of the United States?

2 Which do you prefer A. Hamburgers (B. Yak pie)
C. Chocolate?

3 Would you rather keep a pet A. Rabbit B. Rat
(C. Python?)

4 Which word do you think best describes Christmas
(A. Fluffy) B. Floppy C. Flossy?

5 Do you A. Like children B. Not mind children
(C. Positively hate children?)

6 If you were a Christmas decoration would you be
A. The fairy on the top (B. A small red ball) C. A set
of flashing lights?

7 What is your favourite Christmas present
A. A pair of socks (B. Smelly stuff) C. Orange
cream chocolates?

49

20 July

The application form that's stuck in over the page is the first one to be returned. I don't think that this Mr Bungle sounds very nice. Not the kind of person that I would like to have representing me in department store grottos.

Merryweather said to wait and see what the computer had to say. He fed the whole form into the computer, followed by the photograph that Mr Bungle supplied. While the computer analysed Mr Bungle's choices, Merryweather explained how the computer would use the photograph. It can read all the lines in people's faces and judge their characters from it. It will then produce a new picture of the applicant wearing a white beard and moustache and a red bobble hat, smiling in an appropriate Ho Ho Ho manner. Alongside the picture it will provide a personality profile of the applicant and a suitability rating up to five stars which means they are perfect for the job.

BERT BUNGLE
HO HO HO RATING *****

Application for post in Harridon and Nosey, the famed department store on the Crimble Isles. Perfect choice. Friendly, lovable, patient, light-hearted. A very, very nice man.

Well, really! I think that computer must be round the twist, or the person who programmed it must be . . . not mentioning any names. He just doesn't look right. Merryweather says the computer is never wrong . . . Hah! He's going to get the research department on to it.

21 July
Merryweather says that the computer was right. Mr Bungle happens to be the kindest and friendliest looking person over the age of fifty in the whole of the islands. I dread to think what the rest of the islanders look like!

Here are some other applicants (before computer enhancement!).

Cal Westhorpe.
NEW YORK - U.S.A.
likes: Gardening,
Knitting & kittens.

SVEN HÄRGLESØN
SWEEDEN: likes gardening
ice and reindeer

"BLUE" McHUGH.
WEST INDIES.
likes: gardening
embroidery & puppies.

30 July

What fun we had today! All the best applicants were invited to come up to the North Pole for interviews. Of course, none of them knew what the job was about. There were all sorts of different reactions when they found out that we wanted them to go to Santa University to learn how to be Santa impersonators. Some wanted to go back home on the next plane, some wanted to start right away and, of course, there were the ones who couldn't stop laughing!

Anyway, we've whittled them all down to twenty who will be the first-year intake to the University. We're calling them the class of 67 (since that's the average age of all the students).

THE CLASS OF 67
First-year intake of Santa University

August

Well, they do say that Christmas comes earlier every year,
but this is a bit ridiculous! I received my first 'Dear Santa'
letter today.

I must get out of this northern hemisphere way of
thinking. I was going to say that it's still the middle of
summer, but of course it's not, if you happen to live
south of the equator . . . it's the middle of winter! And if
you happen to live in Tierra del Fuego, I should imagine
it *feels* like the middle of winter!

> Tierra del Fuego.
>
> Dear Santa,
>   It gets very cold and dark
> here. Can I have a Torch,
> some Wooly Gloves and
>   a Grommit please?
>   love   Juan x

Come December they'll probably be in the middle of
harvest time and won't feel very Christmassy at all. So
it's no wonder this young person put his letter up the
chimney today.

3 August

Merryweather says that a Grommit is a variety of cuddly toy that is going to be 'Humungus' this year. (Where does he pick up these strange words?)

He says it's going to be Humungus because the research department has analysed its market survey returns and confidently predicts the Grommit to be this year's best performer.

◄ This is a "CUDDLY" GROMMIT!!

4 August

I was up all last night thinking about this Grommit thing. You know, I don't know how we got it right before we got the computer. Somehow we would get all our staff of elves and fairies into the Ice House, we'd pack up all the presents, put them on the sleigh and deliver them.

How did we manage to get all the right presents to the right children? I've got this terrible feeling that Merryweather has been running the whole show behind my back for years!

Merryweather has ordered, and has stored away in the warehouses, 1,324,902 Grommits. He says that's what we'll need. That's an awful lot of Grommits!

POLAR TIMES

VOL MCMLXIXIVI   AUG 9   ISSUE 40

Santa's Silicon SLEIGHRIDE!

Yes, North Pole Enterprises rolled into the twenty-first century yesterday when their President and Chairman set the wheels of modern technology in motion.

Yes, Santa Claus cut the ribbon and led the invited guests into the new office complex at the Ice House, famed headquarters of N.P.E.

After a short speech he pressed a large red button, marked 'GO', to start the countdown to Christmas.

Mr Merryweather, Managing Director and Santa's Right-Hand Man, spoke to our roving reporter.

'Basically, we at N.P.E. were suffering from information fatigue. We could not keep up with our clients without a massive investment programme. Our whole system is now automated and computerized,' he said. (See overleaf.)

GO TO GROTTO....

SANTA'S GROTTO

CHILD

PUT LIST UP CHIMNEY

GIVE LIST TO SANTA

dear santa

Information sent to Santa H.Q. each present has a code number. this is entered into computer.

when computer disc is full it is sent to the regional warehouse..........

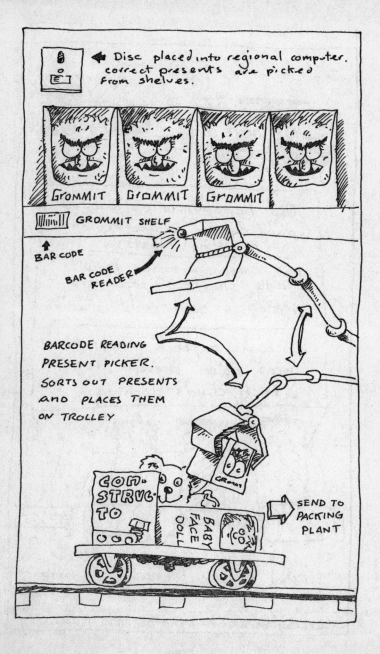

Disc placed into regional computer. correct presents are picked from shelves.

Grommit   Grommit   Grommit

GROMMIT SHELF

BAR CODE

BAR CODE READER

BARCODE READING PRESENT PICKER. SORTS OUT PRESENTS AND PLACES THEM ON TROLLEY

CON-STRUC-TO

BABY FACE DOLL

SEND TO PACKING PLANT

Old newspapers are collected up and dumped at the regional recycling Plants.

The Computer knows how many sheets of paper are needed for each child's stocking.

Enough paper is printed to wrap each present in each child's stocking.

The rolls of paper are then fitted to the packaging Machine.

RECYCLED PAPER PRODUCTION AND PRINTING.

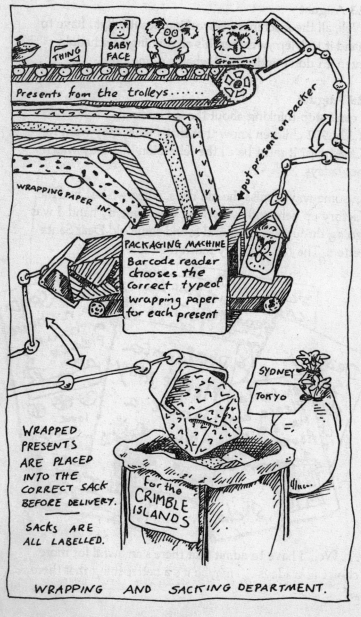

THING

BABY FACE

Grommit

Presents from the trolleys......

WRAPPING PAPER IN.

put present on packer

PACKAGING MACHINE
Barcode reader
chooses the
correct type of
wrapping paper
for each present

SYDNEY

TOKYO

WRAPPED
PRESENTS
ARE PLACED
INTO THE
CORRECT SACK
BEFORE DELIVERY.

SACKS ARE
ALL LABELLED.

for the
CRIMBLE
ISLANDS

WRAPPING AND SACKING DEPARTMENT.

23 August
Well, all the machinery is working beautifully! I have to hand it to Merryweather. It's all running to schedule, even if I don't understand what is going on!

29 August
I can't stop thinking about those Grommits . . . how do 1,324,902 children know that that's what they want for Christmas? It must be all the television that they watch nowadays.

In some ways I miss the old days, when we just had the factory up here and everything was made by hand. I was going through the files and found some old Dear Santa letters. They're all pretty much the same . . .

. . . Well, I have to admit that there's an awful lot more choice nowadays . . . maybe it's a better thing that there is?

September

3 September
Had to take the sleigh in for its seven million mile service today!

They call it 'Wile-u-Wait Sleigh Repairs'! The name's all right if you can wait a few weeks, otherwise it's a bit optimistic. Actually, since there's not much else to do at the North Pole other than wait it doesn't seem to bother anybody.

It is also a fact that when you have a sleigh like mine that does millions of miles a year (not to mention the subatomic effect on its structure of travelling at warp factor three), there is only one person who you can trust to look after it, and that is Axel Rodson. His father, Rod Axelson, looked after the sleigh before him. It's a family business and sleighs are in the blood.

Axel is going to fit in my radio telephone and CD player that Mrs Claus bought me for my birthday. Axel says that since the sleigh is reindeer-driven there is no need for batteries on board, so he is going to fit a windmill generator on to the front of the sleigh for me. Yeehah!

ACME SLEIGH WIND GENERATOR

ATTACH TO FRONT HANDLE BARS.

10 September

GRADUATION DAY!

The Santa University has been a roaring success. Every one of the class of 67 has passed with flying colours. Even Bert Bungle from the Crimble Isles has done well! He may look fearsome but the computer was absolutely right . . . he's such a nice man . . . only goes to show that you can't judge people by their looks!

The student of the year is a lovely old fellow from New York. Merryweather's computer certainly did a good job there. New York is our flagship grotto. Well, they go for Christmas in such a big way in America, and they don't do it any bigger than they do in New York.

It's nice to know that the best of the crop will be representing me in the toughest situation.

We had a wonderful ceremony during which I handed each of our graduating students their new uniforms and a Diplo-ho-homa, which says that the named person has proved himself worthy to wear the red and white and has promised to be friendly, helpful, and will forever have a twinkle in his eye.

As I congratulated each student, I found it harder and harder to hold back a little tear. These wonderful people represent the end of an era. But I console myself that they also represent a bright new future.

The man from Polarkwik ('We make memories from you!') came with his great big clockwork camera. He lined us up and went under his black cloth. He said that we all looked the same except for Mr Bungle, so maybe he had better be the one in the middle. Amazing . . . you can't tell which is me!!!

21 September

Mrs Claus's birthday. Golly, we had such fun! The class of 67 are all going back to their homes tomorrow, and they have been spending their time since graduation working hard, playing with all the toys in the warehouse. This is called research . . . well, you have to know what it is that is being asked for!! We decided to have a combination last night party and surprise party for Mrs Claus.

We raided the stores for false noses and moustaches and were ready, hiding, waiting for her return from work. When she came through the door we turned on the light and all shouted Ho Ho Ho! It took her twenty minutes to decide which was the real Santa!

I knew that Mrs Claus had had her eye on a particular hat. She had been dropping great big hints about it! Anyway, I got it for her birthday present and she hasn't taken it off yet!

Mrs Claus' Hat

23 September

I've been thinking about all this computer stuff of Merryweather's and how every child has presents matched to their requests. Well, I've been going through the records and sometimes it works out just fine when I get mixed up and deliver the wrong presents.

Take Rembrandt, for instance. He kept asking me for a nurse's outfit but I kept muddling him up with another child and kept giving him painting sets. Well, he grew up all right!

Then there was Queen Victoria. Well, actually, she was Princess Victoria when she was young. She always wanted a bumper joke book, but somehow I kept on mixing her up and giving her an embroidery kit. I don't think she was very amused!

Then there was Einstein. All he ever wanted was a train-set, and all he ever wanted to be was an engine driver. So what did I give him? An abacus, exercise books, slide rules and puzzles. Well, it didn't hurt him, did it?

As for Cleopatra, all she ever wanted was Egypt and pet snakes. She got Egypt anyway, but snakes aren't proper presents for little children!

27 September

Off to Wile-u-Wait Sleigh Repairs this morning. Axel Rodson's done a wonderful job. To be able to shift through the space-time continuum, the sleigh has to alter its subatomic structure, so every few million miles it needs stabilizing. No one does it better than Axel.

He's fixed the windmill generator on the front so that I can use the CD and radio telephone. It's incredible sitting in the driver's seat with the speakers on full blast. I'll have to find some stirring flying music for Christmas Eve. Axel says that there will be a certain amount of drag caused by the windmill so I'll need another reindeer added to the team.

WILE-U-WAIT
Sleigh repairs by appointment

Mr S. Claus .... Model *Rasoulopovski Starcruiser MK3 GT*

7,000,000 mile service .... ✓

Atomic re-stabilization .... ✓

Oil change .... ✓ *(2 gallons)*

Extra deer rein .... ✓

Check brakes .... ✓

Fit dynamo windmill .... ✓ *(ACME)*

Fit CD/Radio telephone .. ✓ *supplied.*

Axel Rodson.

October

1 October
YOOP! YOOP! YOOP!

Yes, it's time to go up into the northern hills and call in the reindeer from their summer pastures. This is one part of the year that I really do like. They're such old friends, and it's always nice to see old friends again.

Of course there's a light dusting of snow in the meadows now which dampens the sound of our feet as we walk up to the collecting field. My old horn still works after all these years. It's the same every year. After I blow the horn to call them there is that certain moment of complete silence. The wind drops, the birds stop singing and even the leaves stop rustling on the trees. Then comes the thunderous, heaving, cavorting rumble that is my reindeer coming home for the winter.

The thin, powdery snow gets kicked up by their hooves and floats above them until all that's visible is a giant moving cloud.

The news has got around that there is room for one more reindeer this year because of the drag caused by the windmill dynamo, and the competition is on for that extra place.

They come roaring down the hill into a fenced-in run that funnels them down to single file. It's usually the first twenty, but this year twenty-two, that get through the vet's check-up that get the job. So the first into the funnel is the first to have his annual check-up and have a chance to be chosen to pull my sleigh.

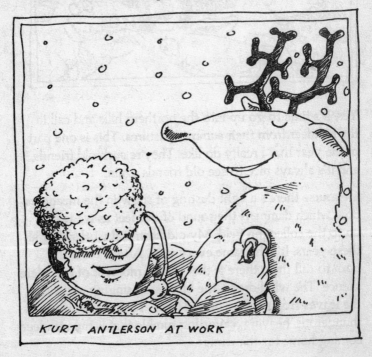

KURT ANTLERSON AT WORK

2 October

Today Kurt Antlerson, the vet, finished his check-ups and announced the lucky twenty-two that will make up the two teams to pull the sleigh this Christmas. Then he checked them all again to decide which two should be the team leaders. It takes a special kind of deer to be in the team. After all, they have to be able to go through warp factor three and out the other side again! But it takes a very special reindeer to lead from the front. Facing the space-time continuum head on is no laughing matter! Dear old Rudolph . . . I remember his nose would start glowing at warp 2.3!

Now all the reindeer will go to the great winter barns at Korgafloë to see out the winter until the spring comes again and they can roam the summer pastures to their hearts' content.

The flying teams, however, have special stabling of their own, they need feeding to build up their strength and training sessions for them to get used to working with each other. They have to be in perfect synchronization to break through those time barriers.

12 October

The teams are working out very well. Decided to take the Alpha team on Christmas Eve. The Beta team can take me out in November for all the personal appearances. It's not quite so strenuous. Everything's working out just fine.

13 October

AAAAAARRRRGH!!! I knew this would happen. I told him! I knew it! I knew it! I knew it!

Four o'clock in the morning, Mrs Claus wakes me up out of a comfortable dream about fluffy white sheep, to tell me that someone is banging on the front door. Could I find my slippers? No! So I stubbed my big toe to find my way downstairs in the dark.

There was Merryweather hopping from foot to foot in a complete panic. The whole system had ground to a halt. The paper pulper, the present wrapper *and* the warehousing system. He'd tried to phone, but the lines were out of action, so he had come over to tell me and take me over to the office himself.

Well, he was absolutely right. The whole place *had* ground to a halt. Merryweather just sat in front of a computer terminal and stared at the screen, its cursor winking back at him.

If you listened hard you could hear him whispering to himself, 'I don't believe it, I just don't believe it!'

Well, something had to be done, so I told Merryweather to start at the beginning and explain the whole thing to me.

Basically the problem lies in the initial market research. It's those Grommits – they've turned into gremlins!

Merryweather has ordered 1,324,902 of them. He got that number from research done earlier in the year. Now, however, letters are starting to come in all wanting Grommits! The computer has predicted a 350% shortfall and that we are going to need a total of 5,962,059 Grommits in all.

Apart from the fact that it is going to be very difficult to get hold of that many Grommits before Christmas, the computerized packing and wrapping system has jammed up.

All Grommits are wrapped in the same size sheet of paper with the same pattern printed on it. That's called standardization. The problem is, that since so many more Grommits will require wrapping, part of the paper printing machine is working full time, which does not allow other presents to be wrapped with paper printed in that part of the machine. So we have presents that need wrapping in that area piling up because the program has panicked!

Now, a program is only as good as the person who wrote it, and we all know who wrote this program! Merryweather and I had to talk our way through the whole problem to clear his mind out before he could sit down and tackle the problem in the computer. I'll leave him to it and get back to bed!

14 October

Dear Merryweather, his whole problem is that he's a perfectionist. He wants every child to have exactly what they want. I had to explain to him, very carefully and very slowly to make sure that he completely understood, that none of us can have exactly what we want! He seemed a bit shaken by this news, but as it sunk in a small light started to glow in his eyes and a smile broke out across his face!

'Ah ha!!' he cried aloud. 'What we require is a need factor and a secondary option program!' I don't know what he was talking about, but within a few minutes of playing on his computer terminal, the building started to hum and the packing department started working again. Merryweather tried to explain it by drawing this diagram. I'm just glad that we're up and running again!

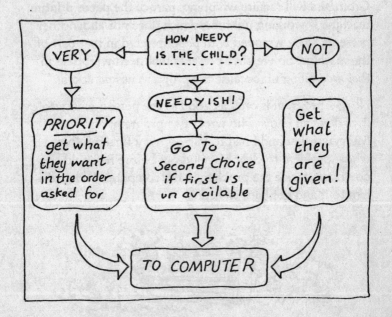

November

1 November

Every year at Hallowe'en, the children come round with
their turnip and pumpkin lanterns tricking and treating.
And when they do, as they did last night, I remember
that today is my wedding anniversary! If it wasn't for
Hallowe'en I'd probably forget! After all, it is a busy time
of year for me and we did get married so long ago that I
can't actually remember how many years we *have* been
married! Sometimes I suspect that Mrs Claus only
remembers on Hallowe'en too, but it would give my game
away if I were to ask her.

So tonight we did the same as every year. We went to
Polapizza and shared a huge, springy, soggy deep pan
pizza with all the side salads and trimmings. Late into the
evening Paolo, the owner of Polapizza, got out his
accordion and started to sing those sad, romantic old
Neapolitan love songs. They always make Mrs Claus cry!
She gets soppy on our anniversary. Tomorrow I'm off
around the world doing personal appearances, so we'll
hardly see one another until Christmas Day.

2 November

I went down to the stables this morning to give the Beta team a last-minute pep talk. I was psyching them up into a mood of grim determination when Mrs Claus came in, huffing and blowing and waving some old red rags around above her head!

'I told you to dry your suit out before you put it away!' she shouted. The reindeer were as surprised as I was and I was worried that she might have upset them. They are very sensitive creatures y'know!

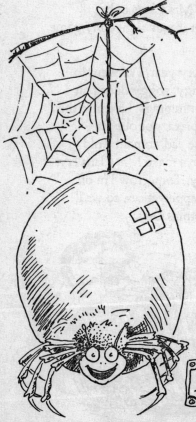

'I told you to make sure that your suit was dry before you put it away,' she repeated. 'Now look at it. Suits like this don't grow on trees you know!'

The reindeer all started sniggering, because in fact suits like that *do* grow on trees. They're woven out of the web that is spun by the Brazilian bauble spider. It's the strongest and warmest known material on earth, and it has to be when you're travelling at speeds over warp factor three!

But it does rot if it's not dried out properly!

Arachnidae Baublae

Well, the upshot of it is that Mrs Claus is going to patch
it together for me. It should see me through my various
forthcoming personal appearances, but I am going to have
to change into a new woollen suit before I actually make
my appearances. Meanwhile Knut Musskusratte, the tailor,
is going to do his best to make me a new suit for
Christmas Eve. Quite where he is going to get Brazilian
bauble spider web from at this time of year I don't know!

The reindeer team of course have had their concentration
thrown. We'll be lucky to get past mach one let alone warp
factor two! They'll be making jokes about my suit all the
way and it's going to be so difficult finding places to
change. I'm sure no one would notice if my suit had a bit
of mending in it.

3 November
Mrs Claus has made sure that I have to change into my
woolly suit! She's patched up the old one all right . . .

with completely potty bits
of material. It looks like a
patchwork quilt!

I've got strawberries and
bananas and tropical flowers!

I'll be the laughing stock of
the upper stratosphere!!

9 November
On our way at last. Just as I thought. The reindeer are completely out of sync. Arrived late in Australia. The only place I could find to change was round the back of the Sydney Opera House! Anyway, worked my way up the east coast then swooped over to Perth and Darwin. Great view of Ayers Rock! Stopped for tea in the warehouse.

12 November
Took in the Pacific Basin today. I love going to Tokyo. All our electronic stuff comes from Japan so I've got a lot of friends there. I never leave without a quick flight over Mount Fuji. There are always new places to go to each year and new things to eat . . . I'd rather not think about what I ate in Manila last night. Reindeer beginning to settle down now – more than I can say for my stomach!

18 November
Africa! The continent full of secret and romantic places. Arrived at the pyramids to the amusement of one American tourist who said he'd come and visit me in Oklahoma next week!

20 November
Milan, Stuttgart, Munich, Moscow . . . It sounds like an advert for something, doesn't it? I much prefer doing the northern hemisphere. Driving reindeer sleighs around the deserts and hot tropical places doesn't get the mood right! Give me cold and snow in Moscow any day. The sleigh runs better on snow than it does on sand!

23 November
Did Britain today. London, Birmingham, Leeds, Manchester and Newcastle, then down to Bristol and over the border to Wales. Lots of little towns to fit in and all before lunch in Machynlleth. Managed to get my teeth into a sandwich but they got stuck on the name! Off to Glasgow and Edinburgh, Ullapool and Kintyre, John-o'-Groat's (because I've never been there before), then Pitlochry for the night.

26 November
Across the sea to the Emerald Isle. Londonderry, Belfast, Dublin, Waterford, Limerick and down to Cork where I can always rely on a warm welcome and a good feed before heading off on the long journey to Tierra del Fuego. Those miles and miles of Atlantic Ocean can really give a man an appetite!

28 November
Tierra del Fuego is quite pleasant at this time of year! Mind you, they said it had only been that warm since the hole appeared in the ozone layer! Young Juan, who was the first to write to me this year, came to visit me. It was he who started all the Grommit business. He's forgotten all about it. He wants a Meccano kit now!

30 November
Well, I got to Oklahoma and the man I met in Egypt was there to greet me. He brought his little grandson along with him. I'm getting a bit worried though . . . his grandson said that he had wanted a Grommit but wanted Meccano now! Must talk to Merryweather on Tuesday!

CAMERA ON REMOTE CONTROL.
AT AYER'S ROCK.

SYDNEY
OPERA HOUSE
↓

Mt. Fuji →

BIRMINGHAM
ENGLAND

Fuji

BULL
RING

OKLAHOMA
↑

MACHYNLLETH
WALES ↙

TIERRA DEL FUEGO ↑

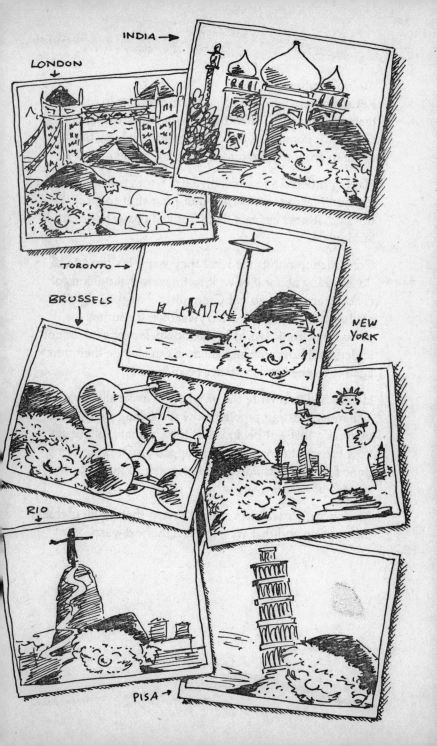

INDIA →

LONDON

TORONTO →

BRUSSELS

NEW YORK

RIO

PISA →

30 November

Returned home today to find Merryweather in one of his technology panics. Now that the grottos are open and the post is coming in, we can begin to predict what children around the world really want in their stockings.

Having ordered a few million extra Grommits and put the Grommit factory on twenty-four-hour shift to meet the demand, it now appears that Grommits have gone out of fashion!

Construction outfits are what they want. It's too late to do anything about it now. It just means that millions of children are going to get Grommits when they didn't really want them. Poor Merryweather. It's turned his perfect electronic world upside down. He says he cannot understand how so many children can change their minds against all the best computer predictions.

He has had to rewrite the program to make allowances. The most pressing problem now is catching up with the wrapping that got behind after the Grommit failure. So now the most economically wrapped presents are being done first. Some children are not going to get what they wanted at all this year.

Merryweather wanders around saying that it's all useful information and that we'll get it right next year!

December

1 December

No matter what they say about travelling around the world, the one true saying is that 'home is where the heart is'. (Even if home is snowbound and shivering at twenty-five degrees below zero!)

Mrs Claus was glad to see me home again. She really does worry about me. She still thinks that I'm too old to be flying around the world in a sleigh, and that I ought to hand the job over to a younger man. She keeps forgetting that it takes a somewhat unusual person to do this job, so I keep reminding her just how much of the work-load Merryweather has taken off my shoulders.

2 December

There is one great drawback to living in a mythical place that isn't even on the map . . . it's almost impossible to get Christmas presents! The polar gift shop isn't much help. The last thing that Mrs Claus wants for Christmas is a

little model of me inside a plastic bubble, that turns into a snowstorm when you shake it.

I really wanted to buy her some exotic perfume called Fission. The advert says that any woman wearing

it will have the same effect on men as a nuclear reactor hard at work. Unfortunately Polachem have sold out already!

3 December

The Class of 67 are doing a wonderful job. These days it is very easy to hire a Santa outfit, put on a false beard and pretend to be me. Goodness knows . . . even bank robbers have been known to do it! But our new Santa stand-ins have been doing a wonderful job. Excellent reports are coming back to us. Hugely valuable information too.

That Bert Bungle, having bounced most of the Crimble Isle children on his knee, has now taken it upon himself to go visiting all the outlying islands to make sure not one child is forgotten. So we now have the complete present list for the islands on the computer, all being wrapped and sacked as I write.

Every time one of our Santas says to a child 'Ho ho ho little girl (or boy) and what do you want for Christmas?' the answer is fed into the computer system back at the North Pole. (Sometimes very little children get so shy they quite forget what it was they wanted, so we never find out!)

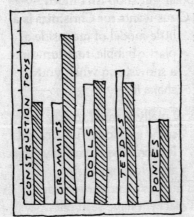

By now we have got so much information in the computer that we can produce a graph to show the numbers of the most requested presents against the amount that we predicted and ordered. Merryweather did very well really.

15 December

Knut Musskusratte came to deliver my new suit today. I asked him how he managed to get the bauble spider cloth so quickly. He said he's had it in stock for some time now. He thinks I should have had a new suit made some time ago! Now I've tried it on I agree with him. That old suit of mine was getting slightly frayed at the edges! I'm going to be wonderfully warm this Christmas with no little holes to let the wind in.

18 December

Merryweather really has done a fantastic job this year, and I told him so today. He got quite emotional and said that he could never have done it without the help of his loyal and hard-working staff. I had to agree, so we decided that when I get back on Christmas Day, we'll have a huge office party in the central packing hall, for all those who helped get the delivery out this year.

20 December

Merryweather gave me a tiny pocket tape recorder today. He thought that I would find it useful on Christmas Eve. I'll be far too busy to write my diary as I go but with this I can talk my thoughts into it and copy them into my diary when I get home.

23 December

Last-minute checks . . . Merryweather says that the Australian and American warehouses are all running to schedule and that I might as well go to bed and get some sleep. After all, tomorrow's going to be a hard day's night!

24 December

Sitting around waiting for the off! Thinking about the time zones is tiring though! This year should be easier, having installed the two new warehouses in Australia and the Americas. Starting in Australia means that I can load up and be at the international date line fresh and ready to go. Then it will be the usual game of chasing midnight.

If you sit and wait on the international date line until midnight comes around, it is then possible to go west fast enough so as to remain at midnight for twenty-four hours. There is no point wearing a watch because a watch doesn't know where in the world it is! This year Merryweather has asked me to phone in every so often to give him a situation report. He says that due to the satellite link we are using, he can tell me exactly where I am, what the time is and whether I am on schedule! That's progress for you! Normally the way to check the time is to look at local clocks on town halls and church spires.

Basically, I have between midnight and six in the morning to fit in the whole delivery. But since I can get twenty-four hours of midnight, Christmas Eve lasts a total of thirty gruelling hours for me. It is all perfectly logical really, but when you have to cover so many miles and so many of them going backwards through the space-time continuum so as to make enough time to fit the job in, the logic of it all is not the biggest problem on your mind!

The main problem with all of this is that if I start at midnight on Christmas Eve, then thirty hours later is the early hours of Boxing Day. That means that I completely miss Christmas Day! Merryweather drew me a map of the time zones and phone-in points. I stuck it in over the page so that I can refer to it as I'm going along.

I've tried my little tape recorder but it doesn't work at warp speeds . . . it uses up an hour's tape in seconds and has run the batteries down in less than thirty seconds. Obviously not built for time travel!

It has just dawned on me that I can't put times down when I write in this diary, since it's going to be midnight most of the night. I go whizzing around the sky so fast that I'm never quite sure where I am!

Having a bit of a problem with those Grommits! The paper printer has obviously been working overtime so that the wrapping paper is not as well printed as it could be, and as for the quality of the wrapping . . . well, I think it has been rushed somewhat. The sticky tape hasn't been put in the correct position, so when I come to stuff them into stockings they become unwrapped. It's most unprofessional! Some of those stockings can be a tight squeeze and more wrapping paper ends up out than in. I'm in a hurry . . . I haven't time to re-wrap presents!

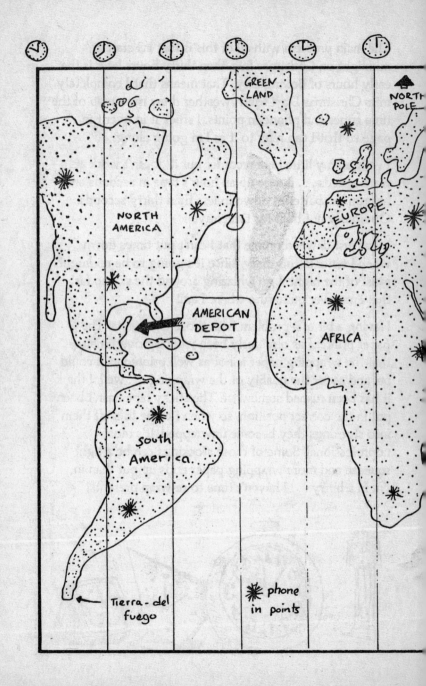

GREEN LAND

NORTH POLE

NORTH AMERICA

EUROPE

AMERICAN DEPOT

AFRICA

South America

Tierra-del fuego

phone in points

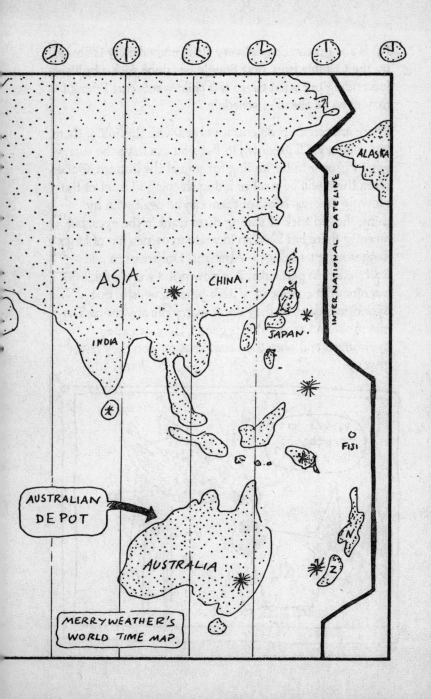

Fiji is always the first delivery stop, immediately followed by the Crimble Isles. Bert Bungle has done such a brilliant job finding out what every last child wants that I think I may even be ahead of schedule.

There are certain problems involved with this job. If there is a chimney, I'll go down it. But you can never be sure what is going to be waiting for you at the bottom. Quite often there will be a cat or a dog sleeping in front of the glowing embers. Most of them can be dealt with by using the old trick of staring them right in the eyes, but recently there has been an increase in ownership of large, dangerous guard dogs – Alsatians, Dobermanns and Rottweilers in particular. I've now got a wonderful little machine that emits a very high-pitched whistle that hypnotizes dogs so they don't worry me any more. The one problem I can't solve is geese! They can't be hypnotized and once they start chasing you they never give up!

When delivering in the tropics there is also another problem. Many's the time I have been creeping around a house filling up stockings when someone starts talking in the room.

The reason I do the delivery at night is so that no one sees me and so that filled stockings will come as a surprise on Christmas morning. So a little voice in the same room as me saying 'Who's a pretty boy then?' comes as quite a shock. Of course it's always parrots, but they can mimic their owners' voices so well that it's difficult to know the difference!

The ocean is a difficult place. There are so many little ships down there and I have to deliver to quite a few of them. Tonight's been OK, but when there is a storm, it is nigh on impossible to fly alongside to let me get on board. Being so close to the water, the reindeer can get very wet from the spray.

Popped in to the Australian warehouse to load up. Phoned Merryweather – he says we're running on time. Must be careful with my diary . . . the only time I have to write in it is when there is a long distance from one drop to another. I get worried that the wind will tear it from my hands.

One thing I have noticed over the years is how bright the planet is at night. When I first started doing this job I had to rely on the moon and the stars to light my way. Now the whole planet is lit up with street lights. The thing that frightens me though is in the rain forests. When you think how few people live in the Amazon, it's amazing to see it at night from above. All the fires burning make the Amazon brighter at night than London or New York!

It doesn't stop at sea. Sometimes it glows! All the pollution entering the seas now can create huge blooms of bacterial soup that glow in phosphorescent shades of blue and pink, but during the day they don't let the sunlight through, so the sea below and the life within it slowly die. Then there are the deep sea oil rigs and fishing fleets which look like small towns floating in the sea with the amount of light that pours out from them.

Seeing the whole of the planet in such a short time as I do really does make me wonder if it can cope with having all these people on it.

Flying across China at the moment, on my way up into Russian Siberia. I don't know what it is that makes people start believing in me, but I'm thankful that hardly anyone in China has ever heard of me. It is such a huge country, with a billion people in it. It would take me until the new year to deliver to all of them. And it's a tiring enough job fitting it all in just on Christmas Eve.

First leg of the journey over. Back home, with just enough time for a mug of cocoa while the sleigh is reloaded. Checked the reindeer; they're all OK. It's good for them to get a bit of a warm-up and something to eat.

You can't beat a northern Christmas. If I've said it once, I've said it a thousand times. This is my favourite leg of the journey. The Scandinavian countries go in for Christmas in such a big way. Just look at this photo I took in one place I visited. They'd left me something to eat and drink on a table all lit by a Christmas candle.

I start to get a warm glow around this time of the journey.
I get all sorts of things left out for me to eat and drink.
It's very rude not to have something, seeing as people
have gone to the trouble of leaving it out for me.

Being in such a hurry I don't have time to check what I'm
eating or drinking. There's often brandy in the mince pies
and fruit-cakes that I have a bite of, and the drinks that
are left out for me are not always milk or orange juice.
So although I only have a sip here and there, when you
add them all up I suppose I could get a little tipsy!

Must make sure I hold on to my diary while I'm writing
in it. I'm terribly worried in case I lose it.

How very funny! I landed in a quiet street on the outskirts
of Stuttgart and bumped into a couple of Santas!

They'd both been to a party dressed as me. They certainly hadn't been drinking milk or orange juice! They wanted to know where I had rented the sleigh! I thought I'd have a picture of us all together. It makes me laugh to think of them telling their friends tomorrow that they had met me and had their picture taken. Since they haven't got a copy, no one will ever believe them!

Since everyone expects Santa to be out and about on Christmas Eve they're not surprised to see me when they do. Of course they don't believe it's *really* me – they think it's just someone else that's got a hired suit and is out on the town for the night.

I managed to wander around Paris without anyone bothering me, and would you believe it? . . . I managed to find an all-night chemist that was open and selling 'Fission' perfume.

That's solved the problem of Mrs Claus's present.

Golly! It's rough out in the North Sea tonight. All those oil rigs lit up like Christmas trees. (That's almost a joke!) The flares that burn off the excess gas dance up and down in the squall.

The Atlantic isn't going to be funny tonight. I can feel the storm blowing up out beyond Ireland. I really must keep a tight hold of my diary or the wind will whip it out of my

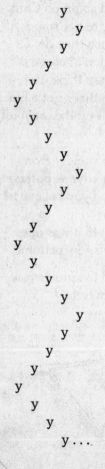

y
  y
 y
y
y
y
y
 y
y
 y
y
y
y
y
y
y
 y
y
 y
y
y
y
y
y
 y . . .

An Important Message for Santa Claus from Puffin Books

WOW – what a year you had! Thank you very much for allowing us to publish your diary. We have kept the original in an extra strong filing cabinet so that it is safe and sound. Do drop in some time and pick it up. We might even have a Grommit or two here for you (and lots of mince pies, too)!

Ed.